KB076702

Forever Together

영원히 함께

Forever Together

발　행 | 2023년 12월 25일
저　자 | Dasom Alice Lee(이다솜), 김민경
펴낸이 | 한건희
펴낸곳 | 주식회사 부크크
출판사등록 | 2014.07.15.(제2014-16호)
주　소 | 서울특별시 금천구 가산디지털1로 119 SK트윈타워 A동 305호
전　화 | 1670-8316
이메일 | info@bookk.co.kr

ISBN | 979-11-410-5926-2

Forever Together

영원히 함께

CONTENT

1st Story   Wrecked Friendship

2nd Story   **싸움왕 민서**

Wrecked Friendship

Dasom Lee

INTRODUCTION

The story is about a conflict that ensues between two best friends, Hana and Esther, over an "accident" that transpired during a concert. Hana is a well-liked and influential young girl who has a vast social network, while Esther is not. The narrative highlights the complex and often challenging nature of friendships, where even the smallest of misunderstandings can lead to terrible misleading.

In addition to Hana, another character in the story is her cousin Hailey. Hailey is the same age as Hana and is a kind and intelligent girl. She always makes Hana happy.

Moreover, there is another character named Madison, who is Hailey's older sister. Madison is going through puberty, which is why she isn't talking much. Muffin is a cute Pomeranian puppy that belongs to Hana.

I wrote this story because I experienced a similar situation with a friend who lived overseas. She used to be my closest friend and we would always study and hang out together. However, we lost contact at the beginning of sixth grade, even though we still attended the same school and met frequently.

I always had a dream of writing my own unique book. This was a great opportunity to write whatever I wanted. One day I want to create a real book open to the public. Thank you, and enjoy my book.

Chapter 1

On a sunny day in Boston, two young girls were playing outside in a park. Hana, a strikingly beautiful girl with a contagious smile, had just tagged her best friend, Esther, who was giggling uncontrollably. The sound of their laughter echoed through the park as they darted around, trying to avoid being caught.

"Okay, now you're it!" Hana exclaimed as she playfully tapped Esther's shoulder. They ran around in the playground, playing tag.

Esther ran as fast as she could, but Hana's nimble legs were too quick for her.

"I'm tired. Let's play something else," Esther panted, wiping her glasses with her shirt. The two girls made their way to the swings and sat down. They both looked up at the clear blue sky and took a deep breath of fresh air.

"What should we do now?" Esther asked, looking at Hana expectantly.

"Hey, do you want to come over and play with dolls at my house?" Hana asked, jumping up and down with excitement. "My mom and dad are both working today; Dad's a doctor and Mom works at a local bank. They both won't be home until late tonight," Hana explained.

"Okay, let's go!" Esther said as she grabbed Hana's hands and walked to her house.

As time passed, they finally moved on to 6th grade. One day, her teacher, Miss Katherine, said to group up with 3 people for the next coming field trip to a camp. They needed three people in each cabin.

Hana was extroverted, which made it easy for her to make new friends and express her thoughts out loud.

Esther, on the other hand, was quite the opposite of Hana. She was introverted and didn't have any friends in her class.

"Hana, I don't want to team up with someone else. I don't have any friends," Esther said worriedly. "I think we should ask the teacher."

"E, we can't do that. We have twenty-five kids in our class! If we ask the teacher, one person would be left out," Hana pointed out. "Don't worry, let's just have fun and try to make new friends!"

"But—"

"Hey, Hana! Can I be in the same group as you?" a voice interrupted. It was the "active, athletic" girl, asking to join Hana's group.

"Sure, Poppy! Esther?" She looked at Esther for an answer.

Esther hesitated then nodded reluctantly.

"Well, welcome to our group!" Hana said, smiling brightly.

'Ugh, it's just getting worse,' Esther thought.

Esther called Hana to meet up early at the playground the next day.

"Oh, okay, coming!" Hana told Esther on the phone.

The phone was gripped between her shoulder and ear. She quickly put on her socks and shoved her feet in her shoes.

"Bye, Muffin! I'll see you later!" Muffin, her 2-year-old white Pomeranian puppy barked back.

Esther was in the playground already, waiting for her.

"Oh, finally! I was waiting." Esther smiled softly and kicked her feet in the dirt.

"Yeah, I can tell! Anyway, what did you want to tell me?" Hana asked, tying her thick, strawberry-brown hair into a high ponytail.

"Well, all I wanted to say is I hope you are my best friend until the end, not with anyone else. So maybe-"

"Yeah, I know! We'll have the best trip ever!" Hana said.

"Ugh, I'm just saying, you're my only friend, so don't always hang out with Poppy and the other cool kids!"

"I didn't know you felt that way, but you know I like you the most. You're my best friend, anyway, and you're super cool too!" Esther felt so much relieved after hearing Hana's words.

"Thanks so much for saying that," Esther said happily.

"Haha, the last one to school is a rotten carrot!" Hana laughed and took off running.

"Hey, that's not fair! You started first and you're so fast!" Esther giggled as she tried to catch up.

The two friends ran towards the school, feeling carefree and happy at the moment. However, Esther's good mood was quickly interrupted when she tripped on a pebble and scraped her knee.

"Ouch!" Esther exclaimed, feeling a little embarrassed. She realized other kids were going to school too, watching her. She felt embarrased. She stood up and hopped to her class.

Hana was waiting in the classroom when Esther arrived, looking flustered.

"What happened?" Hana asked, concerned.

Esther tried to brush the dirt off. "Oh, nothing, I just tripped and fell, that's all." She adjusted her glasses, which were now dirty and askew.

Hana inspected Esther's knee and suggested they go see the school nurse. "Let's get you a big Band-Aid," she said.

Nurse Chamber examined Esther's knee and commented on the size of the scrape. "From now on, don't run on the way to school!" she advised as she applied ointment and a large Peppa Pig band-aid.

"Um, Nurse Chamber? Could I have another band-aid?"

"Why?"

"Never mind. Thank you!" Hana replied politely, dragging Esther.

"Come on, it's not embarrassing, it's cute!"

"Okay, if you say so!" Esther laughed.

The day finally came for Class 8 to go on the field trip.

"Hmm, what should I bring? It's a three-day trip, maybe four pairs of clothes? Just in case? And a toothbrush kit, um, hairbrush, oh! Mr. Noodles!" Mr. Noodles has been Hana's favorite stuffed animal since first grade. Mr. Noodles was an elephant with a fancy black hat. Hana didn't care what other people thought about her stuffed animal.

Meanwhile, Esther was fully packed. She had a big suitcase all to herself. It felt like she was moving!

They arrived at school and climbed into the school bus.

"To Camp Willow!" Everyone shouted.

"Hey, Hana! Over here!" Esther said, pointing at the space next to her.

"Hana, come sit with me," Poppy waved.

"Sorry, Poppy, I'm sitting with Esther," she declared.

"Yay! Hana, you finally came!" Esther said, wiping her glasses with her clothes.

"Let's go!" Hana cheered loudly. "To Camp Willow!" Everyone joined in with cheers and excitement.

After the class arrived, they were greeted by a tour guide named Sir Bubblington who gave them a tour of the camp. He then divided the class into groups and assigned cabins. Hana, Poppy, and Esther were placed together in Cabin Blueberry Bush.

Upon entering their cabin, the three girls noticed three

comfortable beds – a bunk bed and a single bed placed next to it. All three of them wanted the top bunk.

"Let's settle this with a game of rock, paper, scissors," Hana suggested.

Esther ended up winning the top bunk, while Hana got the bottom of the bunk, and Poppy got the single bed next to them. Somehow, Esther was feeling jealous again. Poppy and Hana were sleeping beside each other, while Esther was sleeping at the top, looking at the boring, wooden ceiling.

The next day, Cabin Blueberry Bush and 3 other Cabins went fishing.

Okay, the rules are easy, said a camp guide.

"The Cabin that catches the most fish wins and gets a prize!"

"Guys, I'll go first!" Hana said as she pulled her sleeves up.

"You can do this, Hana!" Poppy cheered. Hana caught a large catfish, but Poppy caught an even bigger fish. Esther didn't catch anything but moldy grass. Cabin BB came in second place, while Cabin Woodpecker won first place, along with the rest of the cabins behind Hana's Cabin. In the evening, the whole class sat on logs and enjoyed toasty marshmallows while Sir Bubblington told them scary stories. Three days passed by quickly. After the field trip, Hana returned home and flopped on her bed. She was relieved that winter break was starting the next day. She heard Muffin barking, and soft footsteps going upstairs. Mom was home early.

"Hi, Mom! How come you're home so early?"

Hana never got to see her mom, Mrs. Kim, close that day.

Hana's mom looked up at her. Hana could see that her mom had large dark circles under her eyes.

"Mom-?"

"Hana, darling, I need to tell you something," Her mom said weakly.

Chapter 2

We need to move. I'm sorry you need to hear this, but it's for a better life. My boss promoted me, and he offered me a job in Canada. I discussed it with him and decided to move. I'm sorry.

Hana didn't know what to say. She just sat there, fidgeting with her hands.

'Moving! What does she think she is doing? Moving, which means leaving my school, all my classmates, and my best friend!' She thought. She couldn't do this.

"Mom-"

"I'm sorry, it's for the best, She sighed and opened her notebook. Look, I found a good house we could live in and it's so nice. Just think about it. You won't regret it."

"I don't know this isn't right," Hana wiped her tears on her clothes and quietly left for her room. She turned on her phone and saw that she got a new text message from Esther. It said 'Let's get ice cream together' with an ice cream emoji. She got ready and walked out of her beautiful home. She saw Esther waiting for her at the ice cream store.

"Hey, Hana the Banana!" Esther made a cringe nickname for Hana.

"Uh, okay? Let's just get ice cream."

Hana chose mint chocolate chip, and Esther, who had a unique taste for carrots and vegetables, chose carrot and apple ice cream.

After buying their ice cream, they walked around the playground and talked about what usual 6th-grade girls would talk about.

"Your crush blah blah, Stewart said he likes blah blah, gossip blah blah, Muffin blah blah."

"Wow, it's already been about an hour!" Esther spluttered and checked her watch.

"Um, yeah," Hana didn't want to tell Esther the terrifying news, but she needed to anyway.

"Esther-"

'Ring!'

"Sorry, Mom's calling! Hello? Yeah, um really?! No way! Impossible!" Esther started jumping delightedly.

"What's up?"

"My mom got tickets for OldJeans's concert!! Esther started crying. She was so thrilled."

"Woah. You're so lucky! Aren't they drawing random people?"

"They randomly pick out a certain number of people for tickets?"

"I am so lucky!! My mom got three tickets for it, but Dad isn't interested in OldJeans, so she said we could go together!"

"Oh my God! Thanks so much! I LOVE you!"

"I'm more thankful I'm going with a friend! I wouldn't want to go only with my parents because they know nothing about OldJeans!"

They held hands and walked home together, as the sun started to set.

The concert was in two weeks, and both girls were so excited.

On the day of the concert, Hana started packing the OldJeans fan wand, wore her fan t-shirt they bought online at 'oldjeans.com', and gave Muffin a big pat on her head before saying goodbye.

Mom! I'm going to the Old Jeans concert! I'll be back home at eleven! Hana said.

Hana Kim! You better be back soon! You promise? Mrs. Kim said.

"Sure, Mom! Thank you so much!" Hana replied politely as she carried her bag.

"But! Finish packing your room. You only have a few things to pack. The moving truck is coming this evening."

Hana said "Okay", then quickly started cleaning her room unwillingly.

Esther was waiting at the concert gates. The concert was scheduled to start at 9 pm, but it was already 8:55. 'Hana, where are you?!'

"Hello ladies, the concert will start in 5 minutes. You must go to your seats and get ready." A security guard who was tall and buff said.

"I–I'm sorry, sir, but we're waiting for my friend to come. Could we stay out here for a few more minutes?" Mrs. Barret, Esther's mom asked.

The security guard looked at them. It was apparent that he was generous and kind. He told them only five more minutes and after that, no choice but to go home or enjoy the concert without Hana.

Esther started getting impatient. 'Why isn't she coming? She promised she'd come!'

"Hi, Esther!" Someone said.

"Who?"

"It's me, Izzy!"

"Izzy? Oh, hi! You've grown a lot! You're so pretty!"

"Oh, thanks! You grew a lot too!"

Izzy Cross was a super cute girl that Esther met in her old Girl Scouts club back in 4th grade. After Hana, Izzy was Esther's closest friend. Izzy had long, straight brown hair that went down to her hips and tiny golden hoop earrings on her slightly tanned ears. She was undoubtedly adorable.

Izzy saw the concert tickets gripped tightly in Esther's hand. "Ooh, are those tickets to OldJeans?! How fortunate you must be!"

"Hello, Izzy! Nice to meet you! I am Esther's mom, Mrs. Barret!" The plump woman smiled pleasantly.

"Hello!" Izzy beamed.

"If you would like, we could give you one of the tickets! Esther's best friend Hana was supposed to come, but sadly she's not here! If it's okay with Esther." Mrs. Barret added.

"Really? Esther, could I?" Izzy looked at Esther with super

cute and large eyes.

Esther looked at her mom. She nodded. "Okay."

"Wow! Thank you!" She received the ticket in her hand, and she hopped and giggled.

"I'm sorry, but the concert has started already," said the security guard.

"Oh! We are going in now! Don't you worry, girls! Let's go, sorry, and thank you for being so generous, Sir."

He nodded as he gave a small smile and let them in.

"So excited!" Izzy said, putting her arms in the air.

"Yeah," murmured Esther.

Meanwhile, Hana rushed to the concert gates after finishing packing and asked a security guard if he had seen Esther and her mom. He said he saw them leaving with another girl, which made Hana furious and disappointed.

The concert was thrilling. People were screaming words of all kinds, and tons were shaking their wands and singing along.

On the other hand, Esther felt betrayed. She wanted to enjoy this together with Hana, but look what's happened now! 'At least Izzy is super hyped, so she's not bad.' Esther thought.

After the concert, the girls had dinner at a pizza place called 'Pizza Palace'. Esther tried to keep the plastered smile on her face in front of her old friend.

"Did you have fun?" Mrs. Barret asked Esther on the way home.

"Of course. The best." Esther said, untruthfully.

Chapter 3

"Hana, wake up!"

"Hana!"

She opened her eyes and checked the time. "3 am?" Hana groaned. Why?

"Our trip! Put your coat on, we need to go now!" Her dad threw Hana her coat. She walked slowly to the garage. It was open already.

"Okay," whispered Hana, putting on her warm, fluffy coat. It was freezing cold. She could see her breath in the cold, dark early morning.

Hana got in her seat and plopped her tiny suitcase with her

stuff inside beside her.

Muffin was in the middle seat, in her fluffy cage. Hana checked the yellow spotted bag just in case something was missing. Muffin's leash, her water bowl, poop bag, food bowl– her food was missing.

"Mom, where did you put Muffin's food?" Hana asked.

"Sorry, what?" Mrs. Kim was upstairs digging for her purple scarf in her messy drawers.

"Where's Muffin's food?"

"It's right here, I'll bring it!" Dad shouted.

"Hana! Your cousin's family is here! Say hello to them." Dad said from the garage.

The car was parked outside, and it was on the side of the road. The small car parked right behind their car. Five people came out of it. Mrs. Brunt, Mr. Brunt, Madison, her younger sister Hailey, and the newborn baby Blake.

"Hi, Madison. Hey, Hailey. Hello Mrs. and Mr. Brunt. Hey there, Blake!" Hana said politely.

"Hello, Hana! Wow, you grew so much! Look how tall you are, so beautiful! You should become a model." Mrs. Brunt exclaimed. Hailey gave Hana a weird look.

"Thank you," Hana said awkwardly.

"You girls stay in the car. We will say hi to Joseph and Lori." Mrs. Brunt fluffed her hair up one more time.

"Okay," said the girls quietly.

Hana removed the stuff on the seats and put them in the trunk, except for Muffin. She put Muffin's cage on her lap.

The girls sat in silence as Hana sat in the middle seat. It had been so long since they met, and they looked quite different too.

Madison had mascara on, along with two piercings on each of her ears.

"You guys changed a lot." Hana said.

"Your dog is cute," Hailey mentioned.

Madison was on her phone. She was scrolling down on pages of Instagram, tapping hearts, and leaving comments.

'Puberty?' Hana thought.

Madison was in the 8th grade, and she was taller than her mom. She had curly dirty-blonde hair. Hana could tell Madison put on a lot of cosmetics.

Hailey was the same age as Hana. She had freckles on her face, with cute glasses and curly pigtails. Hailey barely changed a bit, except for her long hair which used to be short, and her height.

They were close as sisters, and Hana didn't want it to get

more awkward, so she ended up starting the conversation.

A few minutes later, the adults came from their talk and loaded their suitcases into Hana's car.

"Hana, have you seen my purple scarf? I was looking for it in the drawers, but I couldn't find it." Mrs. Kim asked her daughter after climbing in the seats.

"It's in your luggage. I saw you putting it in." Hana said as she sighed, and looked at Hailey. She smirked.

"Oh, I did? Oh yes, now I remember! Thanks, sweetheart."

The car started and the family drove out of their community.

"Hana?" Hailey asked.

"Huh?"

"Do you like your school?"

"Yeah, I love it. But now I need to move. Great, right?" Hana said sarcastically.

"I don't think it would be that bad," said Hailey.

"What?"

"You know that we live there, right?"

Hana gasped. It had been so long since they met, and she had forgotten about where they lived. She thought that it would be so amazing to go to the same school as Hailey!

"Wow! It would be so fun meeting you every day!" Hana

said.

"Yup, and we could be like sisters! Again!"

Madison glanced at Hana and Hailey. She put her phone down and started to talk with them.

They were already bonding again! Hana feeling great thanks to the funny cousins. Hours and hours flew by until they arrived at their destination.

"Guys, look outside! We're already here!" Hana squealed. She could see the streets of New York. The busy city was beautiful.

Hana's dad parked the car and carried out all the luggage from the trunk with the help of Mr. Brunt. Mrs. Brunt was putting Blake in his stroller.

"Hana, take your luggage," said her dad.

She carried her small luggage and her phone in one hand. Hailey's luggage was a big shoulder bag. Madison held a large luggage too, with a scene of Chicago painted on it. Hana also carried Muffin. She barked loudly.

They went into the lobby of the hotel, which was very fancy. Hana took Muffin out and put her leash on. The adults went to the counter and earned their room cards.

"Hana, I heard our room has a significant room! It has a

view of the whole city!" Hailey exclaimed.

The two families separated into two rooms. But Hailey decided she wanted to stay with Hana, so she slept with Hana's family.

Hana didn't expect Madison to come over, and like she expected, she didn't. But it made sense because she was fourteen. She needed her privacy.

Hana suddenly realized how Esther would feel. Would their friendship still be okay? She was worried.

"Are you okay? You look disturbed." Hailey asked. She was so great at knowing how people feel by their facial expressions.

"I'm having a problem with a friend, that's why," Hana said sadly.

"I understand. I had many of those incidents." She shivered. "I lost many friends from fights."

"Well, I'll tell you what happened," she said. Hana told her the whole story. "If you were her, how would you feel?"

"No offense, I would feel a bit mad at her, but it's obviously your fault you were tardy!" Hailey said truthfully. "But maybe she would understand if you told her what happened?"

"You're right. Thanks for telling me."

"For now, you just need to leave all your worries here and enjoy this trip!" Hailey said as she spread her arms.

"You're right again! Okay, let's check out our rooms!" Hailey pulled Hana's arms into the corridors of the rooms.

Mr. Kim opened the rooms for them. The room was very beautiful, with exquisite paintings of the Manhattan Bridge, and the Statue of Liberty.

"I get dibs on this bed!" Hailey jumped onto the bed.

"You know I need to sleep there with you anyway."

"Oh, yeah." Hailey stopped bouncing on the bed when she realized. "But that's better!"

"Girls, wash your hands, and brush your hair! We're going out for dinner." Mrs. Kim said.

"Yes, Mrs. Kim!" Hailey said.

"Okay."

"Are we bringing Muffin?" Hailey asked.

"Yes, of course." Girls, hurry up!

Muffin kept following Hana. It seemed like Muffin wanted to go for a walk.

"Don't worry, we will go in a few minutes," Hana said.

Hana and Hailey went to the other room and knocked.

"Mom, Dad, we're going for dinner. Could you hurry please?"

Hailey said.

"Coming!" A muffled voice shouted through the door.

Madison came out first. She looked extra pretty, with darker mascara and lip gloss. She was wearing a crop top and had her hair in a high ponytail.

Hana complimented Madison, admiring her beauty. "Madison, you're so pretty!" she said. Madison thanked her with a smile, but her eyes remained fixated on her phone. Hailey joked that Madison must be texting her boyfriend, to which Madison responded defensively, "What if I am?" Hailey seemed interested, eager for some juicy gossip. Madison quickly clarified, "No! Of course not!" in a loud voice. Their commotion caught the attention of an old man from another room who shouted at them to lower their voices. Embarrassed, Hana quickly apologized.

The adults soon emerged with Blake and Muffin and looked at the girls suspiciously. Mrs. Brunt asked, "Got in trouble?" Hailey hugged her mother and apologized, while Madison asked if she could hold Muffin's leash. Hana agreed, reminding her to hold the leash tightly. Mr. Kim suggested they head to the elevator, and Hana clicked the button just in time as it arrived. Hailey expressed concern about fitting everyone in, but fortunately, they managed to squeeze in.

As they reached the lobby again, they breathed a sigh of relief, happy to escape the stuffy elevator. Outside, they took a few seconds to enjoy the view of the busy streets and amazing buildings. Mr. Brunt spotted a Starbucks and expressed his love for coffee, but Madison reminded him that they had come for dinner, not coffee.

Suddenly, Madison sneezed, dropping her water bottle and the leash in the process. She was angry, exclaiming that she had spent a lot of money on the bottle. Hailey tried to calm her down, assuring her that it was just a few scratches. Meanwhile, Hana looked around frantically for Muffin, who was chasing a rat that had been eating breadcrumbs.

"No! No, no, no, no, no! Bad Muffin! You come back here this instant!" Hana sprinted fast to catch her puppy.

"Are you happening to look for him?" A boy asked. He held Muffin's leash and handed it over to Hana.

"Oh, thanks! Thank you so much!" Hana said and ran back to where her family was.

"What a kind boy!" Mr. Brunt chuckled.

"That was intense!" Hana wiped her sweat.

"Just lucky that you are a good runner, Hana!" Hailey patted Hana's back.

"Guys, it's a great time for a photo!" Madison pulled out her phone, and Mr. Brunt also joined.

"Dad, not you! With the girls and Muffin!" Hailey laughed.

"Aw, that sucks!" He said disappointedly.

Madison snapped a bunch of beautiful photos.

"Hana, is it okay if I put these pictures on Instagram? Madison asked."

"I guess!" Hana shrugged.

Madison posted the photos on Instagram.

'#NEWYORK#TRIP#BFF'

Chapter 4

For dinner, they went to a famous pizza restaurant known for its cheesy and crispy pizzas. Right after they went in, their mouths started to water from the cheesy, delicious smells.

"Hello, how many people?" A waiter asked, smiling.

"Umm one, two, three, four, five, six-" Mr. Brunt started counting the number of people.

"Nine people. Are dogs allowed here?"

"Just remember, the dog needs to be tied to the leash on your chair."

"Okay, please sit right here. The menu is right here."

Everyone took a turn choosing what pizza they would like.

"Pepperoni!"

"Just simple, cheese!"

"Veggie with pineapple toppings please,"

"Me too! But no pineapples!"

And so on.

Your food will be served in approximately thirty minutes. The waiter calculated.

"Oh! Milk too!" Hailey added.

"Yes, yes, milk too."

After their food was served, everybody was already digging in. Mrs. Brunt fed Blake baby milk while eating her pizza, Mrs. Kim ate the veggie pizza with pineapples, and Hailey, Madison, and Hana all ate plain cheese pizza.

After the yummy pizza, everyone was full, except the kids.

"Mom, please? Cotton candy? Please?" Hailey begged.

"Can I have ice cream? It's best on cold days." Madison asked.

"Ooh! Jumbo pretzel! Dad?" Hana begged.

In the end, everyone got what they wanted. Now they were finally full. They were all happy.

"I love New York," Hailey said with her mouth filled with cotton candy.

"Yeah, one of the best trips ever," Madison said, taking photos of her mini sundae with Hana and Hailey.

"Mmfph." Hana stuffed her mouth with the jumbo pretzel.

""Yeah, thanks to you girls, our pockets are empty!" Mr. Kim said laughing jokingly.

Meanwhile, Esther was thinking. 'Where is Hana?' she wondered. She had sent dozens of messages, but Hana never replied or even checked them. Feeling bored, she opened Instagram and scrolled through her feed. As she was scrolling, she saw Madison's post. 'Is that Hana?'

It said '#NEWYORK#TRIP#BFF'. 'BFF'? Esther was disappointed. Hana had left her and decided to go to New York instead of an OldJeans concert. And she made a new best friend? Esther wanted to ask Hana what she was doing, so she texted her.

'What are you doing?' Esther texted.

'I'm in New York' Hana texted right back. She said nothing else.

"Now she's not talking to me. After all she did to me?" She threw her stuffed bunny on the floor. "Fine, then I won't talk to you either!"

Esther was in a very, very bad mood.

Hana was busy having fun, and she wasn't the type of girl who was addicted to her phone. So, she decided to leave her phone to her parents and hang out with Hailey and Madison.

Hailey and Madison were in the park, waiting for the sun to set while playing truth or dare. Hailey told Hana to sit in a certain spot on the soft, cold grass. Hana felt the cool breeze brush against her face as they perched atop a hill, with the entire city shining below. It was an awe-inspiring and peaceful scene.

When it was Hana's turn, she chose to dare. Madison dared her to dance in front of her whole class when she moved to their middle school. Hana shrugged, acting as though it was nothing.

Hailey was surprised and said, "Wait. You'll do it? Brave, Hana! Very brave."

Hana then asked Hailey truth or dare, and Hailey chose truth. Hana asked if Hailey had a crush. Hailey hesitated for a moment before answering that she did not yet have a crush.

Madison then chose to dare, and Hailey dared her not to use her phone for a whole day, starting the next day. Madison was not happy with the dare and complained about it, but Hana laughed and insisted that she had to do it.

Excitedly, Hana pointed out the sunset, saying, "Guys! Look!

The sun is setting!"

Since the sun was too intense to look at for more than a few seconds, they took quick but thorough glances. The girls captured a few more photos before making their way back to the hotel. Everyone had a restful night's sleep. Hana was worried about meeting Esther. She thought she would be terribly mad at her. She would think of what she would say, next time. She fell into a deep sleep.

The next morning, Hana was the first to wake up. She quietly patted Muffin and gave her Muffin's food and water.

She went to the refrigerator for a small breakfast. She took out a piece of cream bread from the fridge, nibbled on it, and slurped some chocolate milk.

Mr. Kim woke up second. He said good morning, brushed his teeth, and went straight for the shower.

It was already 9 am. Hana decided to wake Hailey up.

"Wake up! Wake up!" She bounced on the bed where Hailey was sleeping.

"Okay, okay," Hailey mumbled. She rubbed her eyes, yawned, and put her glasses on. She checked the time on her watch and was bewildered.

"Why didn't you wake me up earlier? It's over nine!" Hailey

exclaimed.

"Just be thankful I woke you up," Hana said.

"Where's your mom?"

Hana shrugged. "Probably at a cafe with your mom," Hana guessed. Hana's mom always drank a cup of coffee when the morning started.

Mr. Kim came out of the shower with a wet towel in his hands. He told them that their mothers were at Starbucks. He suddenly stopped in his tracks.

"Have you eaten your breakfast, Hailey?" Mr. Kim asked.

"No, I haven't. I am starving!" Hailey said. Everyone could hear the large growl of her stomach.

"Let's get a toast," Mr. Kim said, pointing to Starbucks, "your mom is there anyway."

"Stay here, Muffin! We'll be back!" Hana rubbed Muffin's ears.

As soon as they entered the cafe, the aroma of freshly brewed coffee filled their senses, accompanied by the sound of beans being ground. A queue of people waited to get their morning coffee, gearing up for a long day at work. Hailey ordered a chocolate croissant and a strawberry banana smoothie, while Mr. Kim opted for a bacon, sausage, and egg wrap with a Frappuccino. Hana ordered a lemonade. Hailey and Hana watched as their mothers chatted while sipping their coffee.

"Good morning, Mom," Hana greeted, followed by a cheerful "Good morning, Auntie."

"Hana, today's the last day in New York! Have a lot of fun, alright?" Mrs. Kim reminded her.

"Okay, I will," Hana replied with a smile, determined to focus on enjoying her time in New York and pushing away the thought of facing Esther upon her return.

As planned, Hana and her family boarded a ferry to catch a glimpse of the magnificent Statue of Liberty.

"I know about this! There is a poem by Emma Lazarus, and her poem was cast onto a bronze plaque and was mounted inside the pedestal's lower level in 1903!" Hailey said. "I learned about this in Social Studies."

Everyone knew that Hailey was an intelligent kid. She had an impressive ability to retain and recall everything she learned in school.

Time flew by quickly and before they knew it, it was time to say their goodbyes. The car ride without Hailey and her family was quiet and cold, leaving Hana to ponder over Esther's reaction. She was scared that Esther would hate her now unless she told her the real reason why she was late. Still, Hana was mad about Esther too.

'Everything will be just fine. I know her well enough to be certain that she won't scream at me or get upset.'

Hana was feeling drowsy throughout the entire trip, and her eyelids began to feel heavy. As she dozed off, she heard someone singing a classic song, which sounded like an angel's voice. When she opened her eyes, she saw Esther singing in front of the class in school, which was odd because Esther would never do that. After the song ended, the entire class applauded her performance, but when Esther saw Hana, she started screaming and accusing her of not keeping her promises. The other students joined in, and they started throwing food at Hana. She tried to run, but she felt like she was in a slow-motion video as the students caught up with her, hurling insults at her. Suddenly, Hana woke up, realizing it was just a nightmare. Mrs. Kim turned around and asked Hana what was wrong, and Hana told her about her bad dream. They had already arrived at their destination.

"How long did I sleep for, Mom?"

"For the whole ride!" Her mom said.

"We even turned on pop songs and classic songs, but you never woke up! How is that possible?" Mr. Kim laughed.

"That was a sick dream, and hopefully that never happens in real life!" Hana said wiping her sweat with her sleeves.

Hana and her parents brought their luggage inside and prepared to go to bed. It was already past 10 pm and their house rule was to sleep before ten-thirty. Everyone brushed their teeth, took a shower, and changed into their night clothes. Hana said "Goodnight, Mom and Dad!" as she switched off the lights in her room.

"Goodnight, have a great day at school tomorrow! Tomorrow is the last day anyway," replied her parents.

Hana dreaded the day that lay ahead and couldn't wait for it to be over.

Chapter 5

Hana woke up to the annoying sound of her loud alarm clock. She quickly ate a miniature breakfast, and then got ready for school. With both her Mom and Dad at work, Hana and Muffin were the only ones at home.

Hana took a deep breath. "Here I go," she said as she stepped out of her house. "Bye Muffin."

Hana's hands trembled as she entered the classroom. Everyone stared at her in silence.

"Hana, I heard today is your last day. We hope you have a great time in Canada," Mrs. Katherine said.

"I'm sorry I couldn't tell you earlier, Mrs. Katherine. I will miss all of you guys," Hana replied.

The bell rang, signaling the start of class, and everyone took their seats. Hana stole a glance at Esther, who was reading a book as instructed. They had ten minutes of reading time before their lessons began.

'I should say sorry before something happens,' Hana thought to herself as she sat in her boring English class, 'and she should say sorry too.' The teacher had instructed all students to open their English books, but Hana's mind was somewhere else. She glanced over at Esther, hoping for Esther's attention. However, Esther didn't seem to notice her. Feeling frustrated, Hana decided to write a message to Esther in secret. She pulled out a piece of notebook paper and quickly scribbled a message that read, 'Why didn't you wait for me at the concert?' Hana then crunched up the message and rolled it over to Esther's foot.

Esther looked at the message, opened it up, and wrote something on it before throwing it back to Hana. The message read, 'It's not my fault you were late :('

Hana had written a message to Esther, telling her that she should have waited a little longer. However, while throwing the letter to Esther, Mrs. Katherine caught them in the act. She asked who started it and stared at Hana and Esther quizzically.

Esther pointed at Hana and said that she started it. Hana tried to explain that Esther gave her the letter and she only replied to it. Mrs. Katherine was not pleased with their behavior and gave them extra homework for not paying attention in class.

Hana was fuming with anger when she and Esther had been given extra homework. Her last day of school was already looking bleak. During their breaktime, Esther approached Hana and Hana spoke to her coldly.

"What do you want?" Hana asked.

"An apology!" Esther replied.

"Why did you not wait for me and go to the concert with someone else? I can't believe you! I thought we were best friends!" Hana retorted.

"You were the one who never told me you were going to be late, and you never texted me to wait for you! I didn't want to be late for the concert! You know how much it meant to me! It was an amazing concert! And you're not my only friend, I have a trustworthy friend who understands me! That's why I went to the concert with her! Because you were late! And you never texted me before or after the concert!" Esther explained, her face turning red.

As Hana opened her math book, she said coldly, "Sure. Maybe we're just not meant to be best friends."

Esther tried to respond, but the bell rang, signaling the end of the break. Esther looked at Hana with sadness, but Hana didn't even glance at her. Hana and Esther were heartbroken.

Esther had a terrible time at lunch. At school, Hana was her only friend. Esther tried to talk to Hana, but Hana kept ignoring her. Feeling hurt, Esther decided to sit at an empty table and ate her cold hamburger sadly.

Meanwhile, Hana was still mad at Esther, so she chose to sit with the popular kids: Poppy, Anna, Allison, Alice, Lani, Beth, and Penelope. Hana pretended to have fun, hoping that Esther would notice that she was not sad at all.

However, Esther was feeling lonely and left out.

Hana remained silent for the rest of the day, feeling sad as she returned home. Upon reaching her house, she felt even more despondent to find it empty. "Goodbye, house," she said with a heavy heart.

"Hana, let's go. Get your backpack," Mom urged her. "Your dad and Muffin are waiting outside in the car."

As the sun began to set, Hana sat quietly in the back seat of the car, her gaze fixed out the window. The car ride seemed to stretch on forever, the passing scenery a blur of colors and shapes. She plugged her earphones into her ears, the music providing a small comfort amid her sadness.

The once strong friendship between her and Esther had changed, and the weight of that loss weighed heavily on her heart. But as the car drove further and further away from her old home, Hana began to feel a sense of excitement bubbling up inside her. She was moving far away to a new place where she would be surrounded by family and new opportunities.

Hours later, Hana's face lit up when she saw the beautiful house they had arrived at. It had many features, and she could see Hailey at the window, waving excitedly.

"Hey, Hana! I can't believe it, but you're staying at our house for a week! The furniture for your house hasn't arrived yet, that's why," Hailey exclaimed.

"Wow! I expected something good to happen, but not as good as this! I'm so happy!" Hana said with a big smile on her face.

Hailey took Hana on a tour of the house, pointing out each feature like a tour guide. The house was indeed gigantic, with two floors, a balcony, and a basement. The balcony overlooked a beautiful garden where Hailey and her family enjoyed relaxing in the evenings. Hana couldn't help but feel impressed by the grandeur of the house.

As they made their way through the house, Hailey showed

Hana the spacious living room with a cozy fireplace, the dining room with a large table, and the well-equipped kitchen with all the latest stuff. Hana was thrilled to see that the house had everything she needed to feel comfortable and at home. "I'm so grateful to be staying with you and your family, Hailey. This house is amazing!" Hana exclaimed, feeling overwhelmed with happiness.

"I'm so grateful to be staying with you and your family, Hailey. This house is amazing!" Hana exclaimed, feeling overwhelmed with happiness.

As they walked by Madison's gigantic room, they saw her sitting alone, scrolling through her phone again. Madison paused and greeted Hana with a warm "hi" before returning to her device. It was clear that Madison wanted some time to herself, so they continued their tour of the house.

Despite Madison's solitude, her family was incredibly kind and welcoming to Hana. They greeted her with open arms and made her feel right at home. Hailey took the lead and explained to Hana about the private school they would be attending together. Hana was excited about the prospect of studying in a new environment and making new friends. It was shaping up to be an exciting week!

"You girls will be sleeping in Hailey's room, alright? And Madison, if you need your own space, you can sleep on your own," Hailey's dad instructed them.

"Sure, Dad. We're going to bed now! It's late, you know!" Hailey said, pointing to the clock which read midnight.

"Goodnight!" Hana exclaimed.

"Sweet dreams, all of you," responded Mrs. Kim.

Hana wasn't feeling sleepy, and Hailey was on the same boat. They both made their way up the stairs and headed to Hailey's room, where they had a blast discussing the cute toys, Squishmallows. The stuffed toys were stacked high on Hailey's bed, adding to the fun.

The night was long, and both Hailey and Hana struggled to fall asleep. They spent hours tossing and turning, chatting with each other, and trying to get comfortable. As the hours ticked by, they grew increasingly frustrated and anxious about not being able to drift off. Finally, at the stroke of one in the morning, they both felt their eyelids grow heavy, and they slipped into a deep slumber. It was an unusually late night for the sixth graders, and they knew they would feel the effects of it the next day.

The adults were surprised at how late they slept. Hailey apologized for oversleeping and asked her parents if she could take Hana around town.

Hana thought Canada was a beautiful place, especially since she was living in Ontario. Hailey took her to see the nearby park and school, which were situated a few miles away. As a result, they had to take the bus to reach their destination.

After a few days of adjusting to life in Canada, the day had finally arrived for Hana's first day at the private school. She packed her school supplies, and Hailey helped her with the final preparations.

"Hana, good luck on your first day!" the parents said, giving Hana a warm hug before she left for school.

"I will! Thank you, guys! Bye!" Hana replied as she waved goodbye and walked towards the school bus.

Hailey signaled Hana to come quickly. As Hana entered the bus, she could hear the giggles and chattering of other kids her age. The noise made her feel both nervous and excited at the same time.

Hana and Hailey made their way to the back seats of the bus, where they could sit together and chat. The other kids on the bus looked at Hana curiously, whispering to each other and pointing in her direction. Hana could feel their curious eyes on her, but she tried her best to ignore them and focus on the conversation with her cousin.

As the bus made its way to the school, Hana couldn't help but feel a little apprehensive about what her first day would bring.

Hana walked through the bustling hallways of the school building. She couldn't help but feel overwhelmed by its grandeur. The spacious lockers on either side seemed to stretch endlessly, and Hana couldn't resist the urge to run her fingers across their metal surfaces as she walked. She made her way up and down the three floors, marveling at the various classrooms and facilities available to the students.

Hana flinched when a girl tapped her shoulder in Math class.

The girl had curly puffy space buns and large cute eyes. She was an African American that moved here a few months ago. The girl introduced herself. Her name was Ashley, and she was friends with a cool group of other girls, so Hana joined her group of new friends. Her day was not that bad, and Hana started to feel more positive about her new school.

One day after a few months, as Hana was heading towards the middle school hallway, she suddenly caught a glimpse of someone familiar. That person had brown thin buns with large glasses and bangs. The person noticed Hana and stared and her. Hana's heart skipped a beat as she approached the person. "Esther- is that you?"

Epilogue

A few months later, it was during her walk towards her middle school that Hana spotted a familiar face. She was taken aback at the sight of Esther, who she hadn't seen in years. Hana approached her with a mix of surprise and awkwardness and asked, "What brings you here?" Esther explained that her grandmother's health had become unstable, and so they had moved to the area to take care of her. Hana couldn't believe that they had both ended up in the same school, in the same country.

Despite their past differences, Hana and Esther grew closer than ever before. They spent hours catching up on old times, laughing and reminiscing about their childhood memories. Hana even introduced Esther to Hailey, and the three of them quickly became inseparable.

Finally, Hana's family's furniture arrived, and they moved into their own house, separated from Hailey. Hana was thrilled with their new, incredible home, which was spacious and filled with natural light. She felt like everything was just perfect. She had the perfect house, a perfect cousin, and a best friend.

As Hana looked back on all the amazing things that had happened, she realized that she was one of the luckiest girls in the world. She had everything she could ever want, and meeting Esther again felt like a dream come true.

싸움왕 민서

김민경 지음

제1화

초등학교 시절

어느 마을 자두 초등학교 5학년 5반에 민서라는 아이가 있었다. 그 아이는 이 학교에서 선생님 말씀을 듣지 않으며 가장 힘이 세고 사악하다. 그것을 알고 있는 주변의 아이들은 아무도 민서를 건들지 않는다.

어느 날 민서가 아이들을 괴롭히고 있었다. 그것을 본 유린이가 참지 못하고 민서에게 말했다.

"야! 아무 죄 없는 아이들을 왜 괴롭히는 거야?"

민서가 그 말에 화나서 큰 소리로 말했다.

"야! 그걸 네가 왜 궁금해?"

"왜 내가 궁금하면, 안돼? 궁금할 수도 있지! 너도 그럴 때 있잖아."

싸움은 계속되었다.

"왜? 뭐 야라고 하면 다냐?"

"유린이 너 나한테 이렇게 계속 뭐라고 할래? 나 이 학교 싸움 왕이야. 덤비지 마. 너 다쳐!"

"덤비면 어쩔 건데? 때릴 거야? 때릴 거면 때려봐라! 메롱!"

"와 어이없다! 야 너 죽을래? 너 다치기 싫으면 가라!"

"싫은데? 싫은데? 내가 왜? 바보야!"

"야, 왜 내가 바보냐?"

"바보니까. 그리고 너 애들 괴롭히면 학교폭력인 것 알지? 모르면 지인~짜 바보다. 메롱~"

"야!"

민서가 말하면서 유린이를 밀어서 유린이가 세게 넘어져서 유린이가 소리를 지르며 울부짖었다.

그때 구경하던 유린이 쌍둥이 하린이가 말했다.

"유린아, 괜찮아? 야! 유린이 다쳤잖아. 네가 병원비 내줄거야?"

"내가 내주면 되잖아! 왜 화내? 어이없다!"

민서가 화내면서 말했다.

"네가 더 어이없거든! 왜 나한테 왜 그래! 네가 어떻게 내? 너 돈 없잖아. 바보야!"

"야! 내가 왜 바보야! 그리고 내가 돈 낼 수 있다고 병원비가 얼마 한다고 흥! 너도 다치고 싶어?"

"다치고 싶은 사람이 어딨어?"

"야!"

"재미없다. 그냥 그만하자."

"휴, 그러자. 나도 재미없다. 흥!"

"와! 하민서 너 살인미수냐? 유린이를 왜 다치게 해?"

친구들이 말했다.

"아니거든 흥!"

'내가 그러고 싶어서 그렇게 민 것이 아닌데…….'

그때 종이 쳐서 선생님이 들어오셨다.

"왜 그러니? 얘들아, 종이 쳤으니 모두 자리에 앉으세요."

"선생님, 유린이가 다리 다쳤어요!"

하린이가 걱정하면서 말했다.

"뭐? 병원에 가야겠다. (전화하면서) 유린이 어머님! 유린이가 다쳤어요. 병원에 가봐야 할 것 같습니다. "

"네? 유린이가요? 알겠습니다. 지금 갈게요."

잠시 시간이 흐른 뒤 유린이 엄마가 오고 유린이는 병원에 가서 진료를 받았다.

"결과가 나왔습니다. 다리뼈에 금이 갔습니다. 당분간 깁스를 해야겠습니다."

"네."

다음날이 되었다.

친구들이 걱정스러운 목소리로 유린이를 바라보며 물었다.

"괜찮아 유린아?"

"응. 한 달만 깁스하고 나면 금이 갔던 뼈도 붙고 괜찮아진대."

"미, 미안! 내가 심했지? 그동안 내가 반성했어. 나 때문에 네가 다치고 아프고 힘들었지? 정말 미안해. 앞으로 그렇게 하지 않을게! 우리 친하게 지낼래?"

민서가 말했다.

"아니야 나도 심했지! 미안 우리 친하게 지내자! 우리 앞으로 싸우지 말자."

유린이가 말했다.

"그래."

둘이 단짝이 되었다. 밥도 같이 먹고 놀 때도 같이 놀았다.

언제 싸웠는지 잊어버릴 정도로 친해졌다. 학원도 같이 다니게 되었다.

미술학원에 다니게 되었다. 수영도 같이 다니기로 했다. 둘 다 서로의 비밀도 털어놓았다.

"학원을 같이 다니니까 좋다."

유린이가 말했다.

"나도 너무 좋아 우리 다른 학원도 해달라 할까?"

"그러자! 근데 내일 반이 바뀔 때 반 똑같으면 좋겠다."

"나도"

다음날 학교 수업이 끝나고

"몇 반이야?"

"2반 너는?"

"나도! 야호"

"잘됐다. 헤헤"

둘은 또 같은 반이 되었다. 둘은 학원이랑 학교도 같이 갔다. 둘은 영원한 친구가 됐다. 학원도 더 같이 다녔다.

"유린아 너 안희준 좋아하지?"

"아니"

"아니긴 뭐가 아니야! 너 안희준 만났을 때 얼굴 빨개졌잖아."

"아니거든? 네가 어떻게 알아? 너도 알잖아. 맞아 볼래?

"아니거든? 왜 그래? 너 앞으로 싸우지 말자면서? 너 나랑 싸우자고? 야! 그래 싸우자. 흥"

"하지만 이젠 아니야! 흥! 그래 싸우자".

민서가 유린이를 밀었다. 그리고 바로 유린이가 민서를 밀었다.

"야! 왜 밀어!"

"야, 네가 먼저 밀었잖아?"

"야 그 한마디 했다고 왜 화내?"

"그 한마디라도 조심하라거든! 야, 너 그것도 몰라? 낮말은 새가 듣고 밤말은 쥐가 듣는다고 속담 있잖아, 조심해라!"

"와~~겁나 어이가 없네~" 민서가 말했다.

"뭐 어이가 없어? 어쩔티비."

"야, 너? 하~ 맞을래?"

"맞고 싶은 사람이 어딨어?"

민서가 그 말에 어이가 없어 처음보다 더 세게 밀어서 유린이가 더 다쳤다.

유린이는 병원에 실려 갔고 민서는 민서 엄마에게 혼났다.

그래도 분이 풀리지 않았는지 민서는 끝까지 민서가 사과하지 않고 문자를 보냈다.

"야 너 내 친구 아니었어?"

바로 답장이 왔다.

"그래 친구였지. 이젠 아니지만."

민서는 문자를 읽고 답장을 하지 않았다.

다음날.

하린이가 민서를 만나 이야기했다.

"민서야. 사과 안 해? 네가 어쳐서 유린이가 지금 입원했잖아!"

"내가 왜? 그리고 그건 네가 알지 않아도 돼!"

"흥!"

하린이가 가버렸다.

'나도 그러고 싶어서 유린이를 밀치고 다치게 한 것이 아닌데 자꾸 꼬이는 거지?'

민서가 문자를 보냈다.

"야! 네가 내가 밀었다고 하린이에게 말했지?"

문자가 바로 왔다.

"그래. 그걸 말해야 네가 혼나지!"

"절교하자!"

"그래. 너는 이제 내 친구 아니야."

제2화

중학생이 된 아이들

1년이 지난 어느 날

"유린아, 하린아, 너희 중학교 있잖아. 체리 중학교가 됐어. 엄마는 너무 좋구나."

"정말요! 와 내가 가고 싶은 중학교였는데!"

하린이가 말했다.

"힝. 거기 하민서 있는 중학교인데, 다시 만나면 어떻게 하지?"

"정말? 같은 반만 아니면 돼."

"맞아."

"체리 중학교는 공부를 잘하는 순서대로 반이 나누어지니까 만날 기회도 없을 거야."

"나는 몇 반일까?"

"그러게."

"내일 쌍둥이 아기도 태어나고 첫 중학교도 가네?"

엄마가 말했다.

입학식 전날 밤이 되었다.

"야호! 공부 제일 잘하는 반이라 걱정되기도 하고 설레기도 해."

"하린아! 우리 준비물 사러 문구점에 갈래?"

"다녀올게요."

다음 날 학교 가는 날이 되었다.

"친구들! 안녕 난 1년 동안 여러분과 함께 할 담임 선생님이고요. 수학을 가르쳐줄 이휴정 선생님입니다."

"안녕하세요."

"응! 우리 나와서 자기소개 해볼까?"

"나는 유린이입니다. 저는 그림그리기를 좋아하고 하린이와 쌍둥이입니다."

"나는 하린이입니다. 유린이와 쌍둥이이지만 성격이 많이 달라요."

친구들 모두 자기소개가 다 끝나고 수업이 시작되었다.

"선생님. 첫날부터 무슨 수업을 해요. 그냥 친구들 얼굴 익히고 놀면 안돼요?"

"안돼, 여기 반은 노는 것 없어"

"왜요?"

"여긴 공부를 제일 잘하는 반이니까 공부해야지!"

"아, 네."

"그래"

수업이 다 끝나고 11시 20분 4교시가 되었다.

"하, 힘들었어. 우리 빨리 아기 보러 가자!"

하린이가 말했다.

"그래."

집에 와서 아빠와 함께 아기를 보러 엄마가 계시는 병원에 갔다.

"아가야 안녕 난 하린 언니고 얘는 유린 언니야"

"귀엽다."

"안녕. 아가들아. 너희들의 언니야."

"다 크면 놀아줘야지."

"그러자."

다음날

"휴, 오늘 4시에 끝나네. 중학교에 가니까 수업시간이 길어져서 초등학교 때로 다시 가고싶어."

하린이가 말했다.

"힘들어! 하지만 하버드 대학 꼭 갈 거야."

유린이가 말했다.

"그런데 하민서 몇 반이래?"

"2반이래."

제3화

한 달 뒤

하린이와 유린이가 학교에 가는 길에 이야기를 한다.

"하린아. 하민서 같은 반 친구 때려서 강제전학 당했대. 그런데 하민서 쌍둥이 동생도 우리 학교에 다닌대."

"한 달 밖에 안되었는데 벌써 학교폭력으로 강제전학 간거야?"

"서둘러 학교 가자. 그러다 지각하겠다."

"빨리 가자."

"응"

학교에 도착한 뒤,

"다행히 지각 아니다. 휴~"

"그러게."

"이게 뭐지?"

책상 위에는 음료수와 초콜릿이 놓여있었다.

"어? 편지도 있네?'

유린아. 안녕! 나 너 좋아해.
내가 널 좋아해도 될까? 나랑 사귀자.
　　　　　　　　-하민수-

유린이는 친구들이 보지 않게 서둘러 음료수, 초콜릿과 편지를 가방에 집어 넣었다.

"수업 시작할게요."
"책을 펴세요."
과학 선생님이 말했다.
"아싸, 실험이다."
나반장이 말했다.
"하~ 실험이네."
하린이가 말했다.
하교하고 집에서
"유린아! 뭐 생각해?"
"아 아니 오늘 아침에 편지가 왔었거든!"
"누구한테"
"하민수"
"뭐 걔가 너한테?"
"응."

"편지 내용이 뭔데?"

"여기."

"답장 보내. 유린아."

"어떻게 쓸지 모르겠어."

"그냥 사귀자고 써."

"그건 좀 그래."

"그럼 생각해 본다고 써."

"그래 그게 낫겠다. 그리고 걔가 내게 선물 주워서 나도 줄 거야!"

"다 썼다."

다음날.

"애들아, 오늘 자리 바꿀 거예요."

"야호! 자리 바뀐다."

나반장이 말했다.

"자리 바뀐 거 좋아요?"

"네"

'하~ 하필이면 내 짝이 하민수야!'

유린아 답장 좀이라고 쓰여 있는 종이를 하민수가 주웠다.

유린이는 편지를 주웠다.

하민수가 그걸 보고 끄덕끄덕했다.

"1교시는 지난 시간에 내준 과제 못한 것 끝내기! 다 한 사람 책 읽고 자습하세요."

‘난 다 했으니까 책 읽어야지.’

‘유린이는 다 했나 보네.’

민수가 생각했다.

유린이가 무엇을 종이에 썼다.

 “무엇을 쓴 거야? 줘봐.”

 “어? 아니야.”

그때 마침 종이 울렸다.

 “1교시 끝 다 했니 애들아?”

 “아니요.”

 “음 어디까지 했는데?”

 “이거만 붙이면 돼요.”

민수가 말했다.

 “그래”

 “다 했어요.”

 “2교시입니다. 책을 펴세요.”

 역사 선생님이 말했다.

 “네”

학교 끝나고

 “여기”

유린이가 (하민수에게 뭘 주면서) 말했다.

 하민수에게

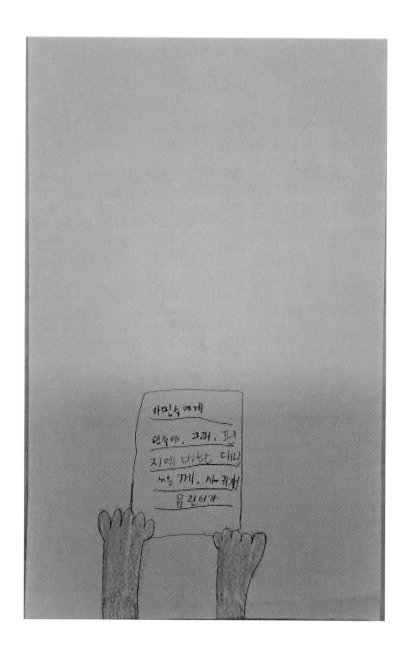

민수야

그래 편지에 대한 대답을 해줄게. 그래 사귀자.

라고 써있었다.

'고백 성공'

민수가 생각했다.

"근데 유린아. 괜찮아 나랑 사귀는 거? 나 하민서 쌍둥이인데!"

"어? 응. 넌 하민서가 아니잖아"

"고마워! 날 받아줘서"

그날 밤

"하린아. 나 하민수 고백을 받아줬어."

"축하해."

"응, 그런데 하민서 쌍둥이 그 아이가 하민수래!"

"뭐 그럼, 받아 주지 말지?"

"괜찮을 거야. 그리고 하민서 그 아이 기숙사에 있어서 방학 때만 집에 온대."

"음 괜찮겠지. 뭐"

"전학을 갈 만도 한데 날 좋아해서 전학을 안 갔네."

"그러게."

"드디어 내일 토요일이다."

"내일은 학원도 안 가지롱!"

다음날.

"아기 좀 돌보는 것 도와주고 있어. 아빠가 편찮으셔서 병원에 다녀 올 거야.!"

엄마가 말했다.

"언니는 기숙사 학교라 집에 안 오니까 장난치지 말고 엄마는 5시쯤 올 거야!"

"할머니 집이 학교 옆으로 이사 왔거든. 아 맞다! 집에 수박 있으니까 먹어."

"갈게."

"네."

"아리와 하리가 태어난지 한 달이 되었어.

하린이가 말했다.

"그니까 벌써 한 달째야? 시간이 많이 지났다."

유린이가 말했다.

"응"

"우리 수박 먹자."

"그래."

"네가 아기 보고 있어! 내가 가지고 올게."

"응."

"다 했다. 먹자."

"곧 있으면 엄마에게 연락 올 거야. 분유 먹일 시간이어서. 냠냠."

"어? 전화 왔다."

"네. 엄마."

"분유 먹이래! 미지근하게"

"응. 분유 만들기 도전"

"분유 가루 넣고 뜨거운 물 넣고 찬물에 넣고 흔들어서 식히면 끝! "

"아기한테 주자. 내가 아리에게 주고 너는 하리 줘."

"잠깐만 미지근하다. 그것도 미지근해?"

"미지근해"

"가자."

"응. 아기 울겠다."

"어! 왜 안 먹지? ,아리는 잘 먹어?" "응"

"하리는 안 먹어"

"내가 줘볼 테니 너는 아리 줘봐."

"아리는 잘 먹네."

"어? 진짜 안 먹네"

"엄마한테 말해야겠어."

"엄마 하리가 밥을 안 먹어요!"

"하리는 분유 계속 줘야해."

"네"

"줘보자. 먹는다."

제4화

데이트와 이사

다음날

"어 전화 왔네! 어? 아빠가 아닌데? 누구지 여보세요?"

"유린아, 나야 민수야. 우리 데이트하자. 응?"

민수가 말했다.

"그, 그래."

"하린아 나 밖에 나갔다 올게. 1시간 뒤에 올 거야."

"어"

"어디서 만날까.?"

"편의점?"

"내가 쏠 테니까 지하 1층에서 보자. 그냥 내려와."

"응, 하린아 갔다 올게"

"응 빨리 와"

"응. 최대한 빨리 올게"

"잘 갔다 와 차 조심하고."

"응"

유린이가 지하 1층 주차장으로 내려왔다.

"무슨 여기로 오라는 거야? 여기서 먹자는 거 아니겠지?"

"당연히 아니지! 타, 유린아."

"어! 뭐야?"

"기사님 고급 레스토랑으로 가요"

"네 민수 도련님."

"뭐야 너 부자였어?"

"응. 가자!"

"다음엔 내가 쏠게."

"응."

레스토랑 도착했다.

"와! 이 좋은 데를 나랑 왔다고? 네 가족과 가지."

"아니야 내가 널 좋아하잖아. 그래서 좋아하는 사람과 같이 갈거라고 생각했거든"

"고마워"

"들어가자."

"응"

"준비했어. 널 위해서"

"고마워."

"이 정도가 지고 뭘 그래. 먹자."

"응"

"맛있다. 그치?"

"응. 맛있다."

방학 끝나고

"하린아. 학교 가자. "

"응. 다 챙겼어."

"가자, 늦겠다. 출발"

"와 토요일이다."

하린이가 말했다.

"하지만 엄마 혼자 쌍둥이 동생을 보시기 힘드시니 집에 가서
아기랑 놀아줘야 하잖아."

유린이가 말했다.

"그건 재미있잖아!"

"그치, 재미있지. 그건."

"아빠 왜 방학 끝났는데 왜 안 오시지?"

유린이가 말했다.

"그러게, 아기는 우리들이 엄마와 돌보고 있어서 괜찮지만, 언니
도 방학 끝나면 가야 하잖아"

"그러게, 그 전엔 아빠가 돌아오셔야 하는데"

"할머니 집이 가까우니까 괜찮겠지?"

"괜찮겠지."

"우리 아기 보러 가자"

"그래, 아가야! 어 자고 있네?"

"그러네! 힝. 놀아주고 싶었는데……."

"나도"

"조용히 하고 아빠한테 전화해 보자." 유린가 말했다.

"응."

"어? 왜?"

"아빠! 저희 방학 끝났는데 언제 돌아오세요?"

"아! 아빠가 조금 바빠서"

"지금 어디세요?"

"아. 지금 미국"

"왜요? 왜 미국이세요?" 하린이가 말했다.

"아빠가 미국에 취직을 해서 미국에 왔어, 한 10일 뒤에 올 거야"

"그럼, 아리랑 하리는요?"

"너희 언니가 엄마와 함께 보면 되지!"

"언니 9일 뒤 방학 끝인데"

"9일 뒤는 일요일이라 괜찮아."

"응, 알겠어. 10일 뒤에 보자!"

"네."

"휴 다행이다."

하린이가 말했다.

아빠에게서 전화가 왔다.

"미안한데 아빠가 한국에 가지 못할 것 같아. 너희가 엄마와 함께 아기들 데리고 미국으로 올 수 있을까?"

"네, 월요일에 학교 가서 선생님에게 여쭤볼게요."

"응, 고맙다."

"네. 이거 가지고 뭘요. 저희도 미국 가고 싶었어요."

"응. 화요일에 보자."

"네"

월요일이 되었다.

"선생님, 저희가 미국에 가게 돼서 이제부터 학교에 오지 못해요. 죄송해요."

"괜찮아. 그럴 수 있지. 지금 가야 하니?"

"네. 지금 가야 할 것 같아요."

"그럼, 친구들이랑 작별 인사해야겠구나."

"네"

때마침 종이 치고

"얘들아, 할 말이 있다."

"유린이랑 하린이가 미국에 가게 되었어요. 모두 들 인사."

"네! 유린아, 하린아, 그동안 고마웠어."

"유린아, 하린아, 그동안 고마웠다. 잘 가거라."

"네."

가방을 챙기고 유린이 가족은 미국에 갈 준비를 했다.

드디어 화요일이 되었다.

"언니 미국에 가려면 몇 시간 걸리고 몇 분 기다려야 탈 수 있어?"

하린이가 말했다.

"미국 가려면 약 14시간 걸리고 3시간 남았어."

"그럼 3시간 동안 뭐해?"

유린이가 말했다.

"일단 밥 먹으러 가자!"

"그리고 비행기 타고 미국으로 오라고 돈 보내주셨어."

"그럼, 뭐 먹지?"

"그러게? 어 저기 돈가스집이다. 저기서 먹을래?"

언니가 말했다.

"응. 그러자."

"언니, 이 돈가스, 진짜 맛있다." 유린이가 말했다.

"그러게! 진짜 맛있다." "언니 그런데 이거 먹고 뭐 할 거야?"

하린이가 말했다.

"비행기 기다려야지 않을까? 왜냐하면, 이거 먹으면 2시간 남으니까 비행기 표 발권해야지!"

"알겠어"

표 발권하는 곳에서

"저희 아기까지 합해서 5명이요" 엄마가 말했다.

"네, 여기요. 어디로 가시나요?" 직원 언니가 말했다.

"우리는 미국 가요."

"아, 네. 저기서 돈 바꾸시고 짐 무게 재주세요, 짐 하나의 무게가 20kg 넘으면 돈 주셔야 해요."

"네, 애들아, 저기 가서 돈 달러로 바꾸자. 그리고 무게 재러 가자."

"달러로 다 바꿨다. 무게 재러 가자."

"응 언니."

"무게가 19kg이야. 1kg만 더 있었으면 돈 내야 됐었는데 다행이다. "

"언니 몇 시간 남았어?" 유린이가 말했다.

"10분 남았다. 짐 싣고 가면 되겠다."

"짐 실었어. 언니."

"응, 가자, 비행기 속으로"

"으앙" 하리가 울었다.

"울지마, 자장자장" 엄마가 말했다.

제5화

미국에서의 생활

14시간의 비행이 끝나고 미국에 도착했다.

아빠는 자동차를 가지고 마중 나오셨다.

"아빠 어느 집이야?"

"저기 하늘색 지붕이 보이지? 거기가 우리가 살 집이야."

"밥 먹을 시간이네 아이들"

"벌써?"

"2시간 지났어."

"응, 엄마가 줄게"

"응, 엄마 우리 뭐해요?" 하린이가 말했다.

"짐 정리하고 다음주부터 학교 갈 거야."

"네? 놀러 왔는데 학교요?"

"2년이나 사는데 학교 가야지. 학교에 갈 준비 다 해놨어."

"응"

다음 주가 되어 유린이와 하린이는 낯선 학교에 도착했다.

"What's your name?"

교장 선생님이 말씀하셨다.

"My name is Hannah."

"My name is Aurora."

"Your classroom's name is Class A."

"Yes, thanks"

교실에 들어왔다.

"Hello, My name is Hannah."

"Hello, My name is Aurora."

쉬는 시간이 되었다.

"What country are you from?"

Anna가 말했다.

"I'm from Korea."

하린이가 말했다.

다음날이 되었다.

"Let's be friends!"

유린이가 Dorothy에게 말했다.

"Let's be friends with me Anna"

하린이가 말했다.

"Yes" Anna가 말했다.

종이 치고 선생님이 교실에 들어오셨다.

"Sit down and open your math book"

"Yes"

다음날

"토요일이다. 나 오늘 새로 사귄 친구 Anna가 우리 집에 온다."
하린이가 말했다.

"몇 시에? 나도 오늘 Dorothy 오기로 했거든."
유린이가 말했다.

"1시에 엄마가 된다고 해서."

"난 2시." "어 그럼 우리 넷이 놀면 되겠다."

"걔들이 우리가 쌍둥이인 것을 모르니까 각자 친구랑 놀자."

"응"

현관에서 띵동 소리가 났다.

"Anna?"

"Yes"

"애나 왔으니. 난 안방으로 갈게."
유린이가 말했다.

"It's been a long time coming."

"Yes, Your house is good."

"Thanks "Where's your room?"

"My room is My room is here."

"Yes, Can you teach me Korean?"

"Of course."

"Thanks."

"This 가."

"가?"

"Yes, me is 나."

"나?"

"다"

"다?"

"You might forget, so write it down in a notebook."

"Yes."

"Wait!"

"Yes."

안방에 와서 둘이 속삭였다.

"유린아, 그냥 쌍둥이인 거 알려주자! 뭐 언젠간 알 거 아니야."

"알겠어. 가자!"

"Hi, I'm Aurora's twin."

"Hannah? Are you Aurora's twin?"

"Yes!"

띵동

" Dorothy must have come."

"Come in Dorothy!"

"Okay!"

"Hello?, Aurora and Anna were here too, right?"

"Anna is here and Aurora is my twin sister!"

"Yes, what are they doing now?"

"Anna was teaching me Korean."

"Let me know too, please."

"Yes, write it down in a notebook."

"Yes" "가, 나, 다, 라, 마, 바, 사, 아, 자, 차, 키, 타, 파, 하"

"가, 나, 다, 라, 마, 바, 사, 아, 자, 차, 카, 타, 파, 하?"

"응"

"응?"

"응 is Korean, in English, yes."

"응."

"Good job."

"Nice is korean 좋은."

"좋은."

"Good job is 잘했어."

"잘했어."

"Water is 물."

"물."

"Candy is 사탕."

"Candy 사탕."

"Now I'm going to check if it's well written."

"Yes"

아이들이 말했다.

"Anna Passes, Dorothy Passes."

"잘했어."

유린이가 말했다.

"Now I have to go home."

"Good bye."

다음날이 되었다.

"엄마, 김서방이 미국에서 취직했어. 그래서 여기서 계속 살아야
돼."

엄마가 할머니께 전화로 이야기하셨다.

"미국에 새로 취직한 걸 축하해."

"하린아, 엄마 심부름 좀, 저기 슈퍼마켓 보이지. 거기서 이걸
좀 사와."

"네, 기저귀, 분유, 양파, 햄, 소시지."

"아! 그리고 네가 가지고 싶은 것 사고 심부름 값, 비싼 것은 안
된다."

"네."

하린이가 마트에 도착했다.

"필요한 것 다 찾았고 이제 내가 갖고 싶은 것 저기 있다."

"This is mine"

갑작스레 민서가 눈앞에 서 있었다.

"어? 하민서? 너였어?"

"어. 바보 멍청이 이하린이잖아! 네가 왜 미국에 있냐?"

"너야말로 왜 미국에 왔냐!"

"난 그냥 부모님 따라서 왔는데, 아무튼 이건 내꺼야."

"그래 가져라, 그건 바보가 써야지 쯧쯧."

"야."

"난 간다, 바보야."

하린이가 다시 집으로 돌아왔다.

"왜 이리게 늦게 왔어?"

"나 마트에서 하민서 봤어"

"이 넓은 미국의 마트에서?"

"응."

"어! 저기 우리 옆집에 하민서가 산대."

"난 망했어."

"하민수도 있는데."

"그러네"

"전화해 볼까?"

"여보세요?, 어 민수야 너 미국이야?"

"응, 어떻게 알았어?"

"하린이가 마트에서 민서를 보러 왔다고 해서. 그리고 난 지금 네가 보여"

"뭐라고? 내가 보인다고?"

"응, 내가 나올 게 너 옆집 하늘색 지붕의 집을 보고 있어."

"응"

"민수야!" "유린아!"

"네 옆집으로 이사 오니 좋다."

"한국에 언제 가?"

"나 여기서 계속 쭉 있어야 한대."

"나 내일 학교 가야 해."

"어느 학교?"

"USA star school"

"나도 거기가. 그럼, 내일 봐."

"응"

다음 날

"What`s your name?"

선생님께서 질문하셨다.

"My name is Mila."

민서가 말했다.

"My name is Mason."

민수가 말했다.

"Mila is class B, mason is class A"

"Thanks"

"Hi. My name is Mason"

"Mason sat down next to Hannah in his seat!"

"Yes"

쉬는 시간이 되었다.

"Dorothy, have you studied Korean?"

유린이가 말했다.

"응"

도로시가 말했다.

"You speak Korean well."

민수가 말했다.

"You're welcome."

그날 저녁 영상통화

"Anna, have you studied korean?"

"응, 공부했어."

"That's not what I'm telling you. How did you know?"

"I studied it out of curiosity."

"잘했어."

"today, I'm going to learn what's in the class."

"응"

"Computer is 컴퓨터. textbook is 교과서"

"Two things are important, memorize them or write them in a notebook"

"응."

다음 날.

"와! 바다다."

"엄마는 왜 지금 여행 와?" 언니가 말했다.

"지금이 딱 좋은 날씨야."

"응"

"나 그럼 학교 빠지는 거야?"

"응, 지금 많이 놀고 학교는 내일모레 가지 뭐."

"지금 재미있게 놀자."

"와! 배 많다."

"여긴 항구인가 봐."

"어 민서도 없으니까, 너무 기분이 좋다."

"그러게"

"난 빨리 얘들 한국어 가르쳐 주고 싶어."

"그거 진짜 재미있어."

"엄마 아빠 벌써 저기까지 갔어?"

"그러네. 정말 빨라."

"지금쯤 얘들 학교 끝났겠다."

"내일 점심 맛있는 건데."

"힝, 그래도 맛있는 것 먹을 수 있잖아."

"그건 맞아,"

"엄마한테 수박 주스 먹자고 하자."

"그래"

"아기들 밥 먹을 시간이다. 기저귀도 갈아줘야 해."

"엄마한테 일을 다하고 나면 주스 사달라고 해야지. "

"나도."

"언니는?"

"난 초코 우유. 왠지 오늘은 초콜릿을 먹고 싶어."

"알겠어."

다음 날
"엄마, 오늘 워터파크 가는 것 맞죠?" 하린이가 말했다.
"응, 일단 갈 준비해, 워터파크에 갈 준비."
"네"
"근데 아리랑 하리는요?"
"할머니가 봐주실 거야."
"네"
Water park
"5 people"
"Yes, it's a water park, right?"
직원이 말했다.
"Yes"
"슬라이드 타자!"
하린이가 말했다.
"무서워서 타기 싫어."
유린이가 말했다.
"그래도 타자! 응?"
"음. 타자."
"가자."
"엄마 저희 저 작은 슬라이드 타고 올게요."
"응, 바로 와야 해."

"네."

"가자."

슬라이드를 많이 타고 많이 놀고 다음 날

"I'm going to change seats"

선생님이 말했다.

"Yes"

"Let's go to this spot."

하린이는 애나, 유린이는 도로시와 짝이 됐다.

"I have a bunch of homework assignments."

"I don't like it" "I need to do some research on
Korean."

"Yes"

쉬는 시간이 되었다.

"Can you do your homework today?"

"Yes"

"Mason was transferred to the school."

'어 민수 온 지 얼마 안되었었는데'

"민수야 너 이사가?"

"응, 하민서가 이사하라고 하잖아"

"안녕"

"응 안녕"

민서와 유린이는 끝까지 화해하지 않고 헤어졌다.

유린이는 민서가 가는 것은 좋아했는데 민수가 한국에 가니까 슬퍼했다. 유린이랑 하린이는 미국에서 행복하게 살았다.

작가의 말

저는 한 5학년 때 학원에서 놀림을 받았습니다.

그때 유린이처럼 저를 위로해주고 도와주는 친구가 나타나서 든든했습니다.

그건 몇 년 전의 일이라 지금은 그 학원을 다니지 않습니다.

언젠간 그 친구한테 나도 도와줄 것입니다. 여러분도 힘들어하는 아이들을 도와주면 뿌듯할 것입니다. 그 친구도 분명히 뿌듯했을 것입니다. 여러분은 민서처럼 되지 말고 유린이처럼 삽시다.